American Lives

Abraham Lincoln

Rick Burke

Heinemann Library
Chicago, Illinois

© 2003 Heinemann Library
a division of Reed Elsevier Inc.
Chicago, Illinois

Customer Service 888-454-2279

Visit our website at www.heinemannlibrary.com

Created by the publishing team
at Heinemann Library

Designed by Ginkgo Creative, Inc.
Photo Research by Kathryn Creech
Printed and Bound in the United States by
Lake Book Manufacturing, Inc.

07 06
10 9 8 7 6 5 4

Library of Congress Cataloging-in-Publication Data
Burke, Rick, 1957-
  Abraham Lincoln / Rick Burke.
     p. cm. — (American lives)
Summary: A biography of the Illinois lawyer who
served the country as president through the
difficulties of the Civil War.
Includes bibliographical references and index.
  ISBN 1-40340-155-1 ((lib. bdg.)) —
  ISBN 1-40340-411-9 ((pbk.))
  1. Lincoln, Abraham, 1809-1865—Juvenile
literature. 2. Presidents—United States—
Biography—Juvenile literature. [1. Lincoln,
Abraham, 1809-1865. 2. Presidents.] I. Title.
  E457.905 .B87 2002
  973.7'092—dc21
                    2002004556

Acknowledgments
The author and publishers are grateful to the
following for permission to reproduce copyright
material: pp. 4, 7, 10, 11, 19, 25 The Library of
Congress; p. 6 SEF/Art Resource; p. 8L Abraham
Lincoln Library and Museum, Lincoln Memorial
University, Harrowgate, Tennessee; p. 8R Chicago
Historical Society; p. 9 North Wind Picture
Archives; pp. 12, 14, 15, 17, 22, 23, 24, 26 Corbis;
p. 13 The Granger Collection, New York; p. 18
National Portrait Gallery, Smithsonian Institution/
Art Resource; p. 20 Minnesota Historical Society/
Corbis; p. 21 Index Stock; p. 27 Hulton Archive/
Getty Images; p. 28 Izzy Schwartz/PhotoDisc; p. 29
R. Morley/PhotoLink/PhotoDisc

Cover photograph: Bettmann/Corbis

Special thanks to Patrick Halladay for his help in
the preparation of this book. Rick Burke thanks
Sherry . . . you're as memorable as A. Lincoln.

Every effort has been made to contact copyright
holders of any material reproduced in this book.
Any omissions will be rectified in subsequent
printings if notice is given to the publisher.

Some words are shown in bold, **like this.** You can
find out what they mean by looking in the glossary.

For more information on the image of Abraham Lincoln
that appears on the cover of this book, turn to page 15.

Contents

A President's Journey

Abraham Lincoln had just been elected the president of the United States. He was riding a train from his home in Springfield, Illinois, to Washington, D.C., in February 1861.

It wouldn't be an easy trip. There were people along the way who wanted to kill Lincoln. He was facing the biggest problem any president had ever had to deal with.

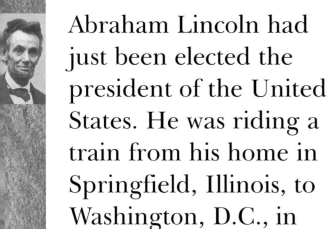

This photograph of Lincoln was taken four days before he died in April 1865.

The people of the southern states wanted to leave the United States. They thought that Lincoln would end **slavery.** They said they needed slaves to help grow crops like tobacco and cotton.

The people of the northern states thought slavery was wrong. Leaders in the South decided to leave the United States and start their own country. They called it the **Confederate** States of America.

Patriots had fought British soldiers almost 100 years earlier to make the United States a free country. Lincoln wanted to honor them by keeping the country together. It would be hard to do.

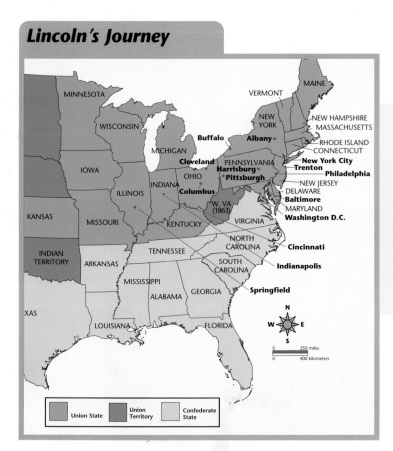

Lincoln's Journey

In 1861, Lincoln stopped in these cities on his twelve-day train journey from Springfield to Washington, D.C.

Growing Up

Abraham Lincoln was born in a one-room log cabin on February 12, 1809, in Hardin County, Kentucky. He was named after his grandfather.

Abraham was the second child born to Thomas and Nancy Lincoln. Abraham's older sister, Sarah, was born in 1807.

The Lincoln family was poor. Thomas Lincoln was a farmer. Like other farmers, he

This cabin was built in 1931 on the site of Lincoln's boyhood home in Kentucky.

needed his children to help in the fields. Not everyone went to school when Abraham was a child. Abraham's parents couldn't read or write.

The Life of Abraham Lincoln

1809	1834	1842	1846
Born in Kentucky on February 12.	*Elected to **Illinois House of Representatives**.*	*Married Mary Todd on November 4.*	*Elected to U.S. House of Representatives.*

Sometimes Abraham and Sarah were allowed to go to school. Abraham loved to learn. He would read books whenever he could. When he plowed his father's fields, he would take a break after each row he plowed. He would read a few lines while the horse rested.

Abraham sat by the fire in the cabin so he could read at night.

Lincoln Firsts

- *First president to be born in Kentucky.*
- *First and only president to receive a **patent**.*
- *First **Republican** to be elected president.*

1860	1864	1865	1865
Elected 16th president of the United States on November 6.	*Reelected president on November 8.*	*Shot by John Wilkes Booth on April 14.*	*Died on April 15 in Washington, D.C.*

New Places to Live

Thomas Lincoln moved his family to Little Pigeon Creek, Indiana, when Abraham was seven years old. He was just nine years old when his mother died. A year later, Thomas married a woman everyone called Sally. Sally was a **widow** with three children of her own. She loved Abraham and Sarah, and they loved her.

Abraham was good with an ax. He cut down trees for his father, split logs, made fences, and chopped firewood. He grew tall and strong, but he learned that he didn't really like being a farmer.

Thomas Lincoln and his second wife, Sarah "Sally" Bush Johnston, were married on December 2, 1819.

Lincoln guided a boat like this one, called a flatboat, down the Mississippi River.

In 1830, when Abraham was 21 years old, Thomas moved the family again. This time, they moved just west of the city of Decatur, Illinois. Abraham helped build a cabin and clear land to farm.

After he was finished, Abraham moved away. He worked on a boat that traveled down the Mississippi River to the city of New Orleans. He also found a home in New Salem, Illinois.

Land of Lincoln

In 1834, Lincoln was elected to the **Illinois House of Representatives.** *"Land of Lincoln" is the state slogan.*

9

Law and Mary

Lincoln's friend John Todd Stuart told him he should become a lawyer. Lincoln took a bag full of law books to New Salem to study. On nice days, he would sit against a tree and read books all day long.

After three years of studying, Lincoln passed the test to become a lawyer. He moved to Springfield, Illinois, to be a lawyer. He was a good lawyer there. During a **trial,** a witness said he saw Lincoln's **client** kill someone by the light of the full moon. Lincoln brought an **almanac** that showed the moon was not bright that night. He saved his client from jail.

This may be the earliest photo of Lincoln, taken in 1846 or 1847.

Mary Todd was 23 when she married Lincoln, who was 33.

In December 1839, Lincoln went to a friend's party in Springfield. He liked being around people, but talking to women made him nervous. He worried that he would say or do something wrong or rude.

At the party, Lincoln met a young woman from Lexington, Kentucky. She was named Mary Todd. They liked each other right away. Mary's parents didn't want her to marry Lincoln, but the two got married anyway on November 4, 1842. They had four boys— Robert, Edward, William, and Tad—but only Robert lived to be an adult.

Lincoln-Douglas Debates

In 1858, Lincoln tried to get elected as a **senator** of Illinois because he didn't like **slavery.** Lincoln thought that if slavery were kept just in the southern states then the practice of owning people would go away.

The other **candidate** in the election was Stephen Douglas. He thought that people living in areas that became new states should decide for themselves whether to allow slavery. Lincoln challenged Douglas to seven **debates.** This way, each man could explain his ideas.

Douglas supported Lincoln when Lincoln became president and when the **Civil War** began.

Tall and Small

Lincoln and Douglas looked strange standing next to each other during the debates. Douglas was only five-foot-four (1.65 meters), while Lincoln was a foot taller. Douglas had the nickname "Little Giant."

The debates were held in seven different cities in Illinois. Thousands of people came to hear Douglas and Lincoln speak. Newspapers all over the United States printed what each man said. Lincoln's ideas about ending slavery made people in the South angry and nervous.

As the debates went on, Douglas's low voice became worn out and hard to hear. Lincoln, who had a higher voice, could still be heard.

Election

Douglas won the election for **senator.** But Lincoln's ideas and words made him famous all over the United States.

In 1860, Lincoln tried to get elected to be president of the United States. The other **candidates** were Douglas, John Bell from Tennessee, and John Breckinridge of Kentucky. The people who didn't want Lincoln to be president split up their votes between the three other candidates. As a result, Lincoln had the most votes and won the election.

This election poster shows Lincoln and the candidate for vice president, Hannibal Hamlin.

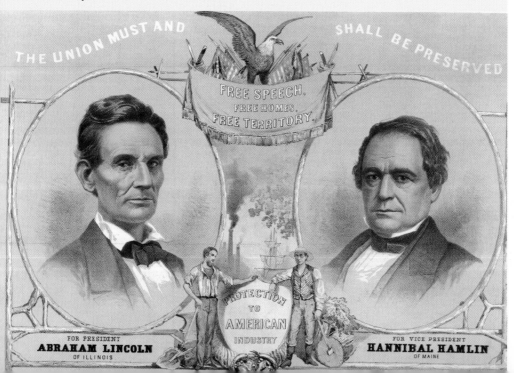

These pictures show Lincoln before he had a beard and after he grew one.

Just before Election Day, Lincoln got a letter from an eleven-year-old girl named Grace Bedell from Westfield, New York. Grace asked Lincoln to grow a beard. She thought Lincoln would look better with a beard because his face was so thin. She also said that women all over the country would get their husbands to vote for Lincoln if he had a beard. Lincoln grew a beard and kept it for the rest of his life.

Mr. Lincoln

Lincoln hated the name Abe. He liked people to call him Lincoln or Mr. Lincoln. Mrs. Lincoln called him "Father," and he called her "Mother."

A Nation Split

Lincoln became president in 1861. Some southern states had already left the U.S. to form the **Confederate** States of America. About nine million people, including four million **slaves,** lived in those states. Confederate leaders wanted all U.S. government offices and soldiers out of the Confederate states. Lincoln refused. He wouldn't give in without a fight.

Twenty-three states with about 22 million people stayed in the U.S. These states had more factories and railroads, but the South had more generals to lead soldiers into battle.

Union and Confederate States

This picture shows the Confederate attack on Fort Sumter in South Carolina, the first battle of the Civil War.

On April 12, 1861, the Confederates attacked a United States fort in Charleston, South Carolina. The **Civil War** had begun. Lincoln didn't have very good luck picking a general to lead **Union** soldiers in the war. He wanted Robert E. Lee to be his general, but Lee loved his home state of Virginia, a southern state. Lee later led Confederate soldiers.

Lincoln picked Irvin McDowell as his general, but McDowell wasn't a good choice. Lincoln tried many generals until he found one who knew how to fight well.

Freeing the Slaves

At the beginning of the **Civil War,** Lincoln said he would let the South keep their **slaves.** But the southern states told Lincoln they wouldn't come back to the United States unless slavery was allowed in every state.

Lincoln didn't want that to happen, but he did want to stop the war. He wanted to save the **Union.** If that meant freeing no slaves, all slaves, or some slaves, Lincoln said he would do it. He wanted the United States to stay as one united country. The South was not willing to give in, so Lincoln made a decision.

This photo of Lincoln was taken in 1863, the same year he signed the Emancipation Proclamation.

This version of one of the pages of the proclamation features some of Lincoln's own handwriting.

On January 1, 1863, Lincoln signed the **Emancipation Proclamation.** This document said that all slaves living in the states at war with the Union were now free. Lincoln said, "If my name ever goes down in history, it will be for this act."

However, the slaves in the states of Missouri, Kentucky, Maryland, and Delaware would still be slaves. Lincoln didn't free the slaves in those states because he wanted the states to stay in the Union.

Gettysburg Address

Early in the **Civil War,** the **Union** didn't do very well in its battles. But the war began to go better for the Union at the Battle of Gettysburg in July 1863. General Robert E. Lee and his **Confederate** soldiers traveled into Gettysburg, Pennsylvania, hoping to find shoes for the soldiers.

General George Meade and his Union soldiers met Lee's army near Gettysburg. After three days of bloody fighting, the Union soldiers made the Confederates withdraw.

At Gettysburg, Meade had thousands more soldiers than Lee did.

About 50,000 soldiers died at the Battle of Gettysburg. Part of the land there was used to bury the dead, and it became a national soldier's cemetery. On November 19, 1863, Edward Everett, a famous speaker, gave a speech at the cemetery. Lincoln was also invited to speak.

This is what the Gettysburg National Cemetery looks like today.

Everett spoke for over two hours. When it was Lincoln's turn to speak, he took out two sheets of paper and read ten sentences he had written. In beautiful, simple language, he told why the United States needed to be kept as one nation. The speech, now known as the Gettysburg Address, is one of the most famous in American history.

Finding a General

Lincoln didn't know anything about leading an army when he was elected president. At the beginning of the war, he trusted his generals to know what they were supposed to do. The problem was that his generals weren't very good.

Lincoln is seen here with his son Tad. Tad liked to play tricks on other people when the Lincolns lived in the White House.

Lincoln learned about leading an army the same way he learned about everything else. He read. Lincoln knew that the **Union** had more people and was twice as big as the **Confederate** states. The way to win the war was to fight the southern armies as often as possible. The Union needed to fight until the South had no more men left to fight.

Lincoln finally found a general who thought the same way he did. He picked Ulysses S. Grant to lead the Union soldiers. Grant had won battles for the Union in the western part of the country. Unlike Lincoln's other generals, Grant wasn't afraid to fight.

Grant wanted to find and attack the Confederates until they quit. Grant sent General William Tecumseh Sherman south to Georgia and up through South and North Carolina. Grant hoped to catch the South's army between two huge Union armies.

This picture of General Grant was taken near a battlefield in the state of Virginia.

Reelection

Lincoln could see that the war was almost over. The factories, railroads, money, and population of the North were just too much for the South to keep up with. He wanted to win the war, but he also wanted the southern states to rejoin the United States.

In November 1864, Lincoln wanted to be elected president again. This time he faced George B. McClellan, a man Lincoln fired as general of one of the main **Union** armies.

This picture shows Lincoln at a meeting in 1862 with McClellan and other soldiers on a battlefield in the state of Maryland.

A huge crowd showed up in Washington, D.C., to see Lincoln start his second term as president.

It looked like Lincoln might not win the election. The people of the North were tired of the war. Thousands of men had died. McClellan told voters that if he was elected, he would end the war. The war went Lincoln's way right before Election Day.

Union soldiers captured Atlanta, Georgia, and the **Confederate** navy was destroyed in Mobile Bay, Alabama. Lincoln won the election by about 400,000 votes. More than four million men voted in the election. On April 9, 1865, General Lee gave up fighting for the South. The war had ended.

Gunshot

In early April 1865, Lincoln had a dream that he told some people about. In the dream, he was walking in the White House one night. He saw a dead body and asked a nearby soldier who had died. The soldier said that someone had just killed the president. The dream scared Lincoln, but he joked about it like he often did when something scared him.

On the night of April 14, 1865, Lincoln and his wife, Mary, went to Ford's Theatre in Washington, D.C., to see a play called *Our American Cousin*. When they entered the theater, the crowd stood up and clapped. The president smiled, waved, and sat down in a seat overlooking the stage.

This picture of the outside of Ford's Theatre was taken in the 1870s.

Booth, a well-known actor of the time, was shot while soldiers were trying to catch him.

About an hour later, a man named John Wilkes Booth crept up the stairs to where Lincoln was sitting. He pulled a gun from his coat and shot Lincoln in the back of the head. Doctors in the theater took Lincoln to a house across the street. Lincoln died early the next morning.

Lincoln's Guard

Lincoln had a guard with him at Ford's Theatre. The guard was supposed to sit near the president, but the guard left his seat.

Remembering Lincoln

The United States and the rest of the world remember Lincoln as one of the country's greatest presidents. He was born in a log cabin and went to school for only about a year. But through hard work, he taught himself the lessons he needed to succeed.

Lincoln proved that people who didn't have much could grow up to be president. He faced the biggest problem any American president had ever seen. He held a nation together when it was splitting in half. Lincoln gave millions of **slaves** something they never thought they would have—their freedom.

The Lincoln Memorial in Washington, D.C., was finished in 1922.

This statue is located in the entrance to the Memorial, which was built as a reminder of what Lincoln did for his country.

Lincoln gave strength and leadership to a nation when people needed it the most. His words and actions gave people the courage to fight for what they believed in. They fought to keep a nation as one and to put an end to slavery. Many people didn't like Lincoln because of his beliefs. But that didn't matter to him. Lincoln always tried to have the courage to do what he thought was right for the United States of America.

Glossary

almanac book put out each year that has a calendar and weather forecasts and lists facts about ocean tides, sunsets, and sunrises

candidate person who wants to be elected to an office, position, or job

Civil War war between the northern and southern states that lasted from 1861 to 1865

client person who hires someone for advice and help

Confederate person who was on the side of the eleven states that formed the Confederate States of America. During the Civil War, the states were also known as the South.

debate to argue for or against an idea

Emancipation Proclamation document that in 1862 promised freedom to any slaves living in Confederate states that did not rejoin the Union

Illinois House of Representatives part of the state government that makes the laws for Illinois

patent right of an inventor to make, use, or sell his invention

patriot person who loves his or her country

Republican member of the Republican Party, one of the two major political groups in the United States

senator member of U.S. Senate, one of the main lawmaking organizations in the United States

slavery when one person is owned by another

trial hearing in a court of law to decide something

Union side that fought for the states that stayed as part of the United States during the Civil War. Also known as the North.

widow woman whose husband has died

More Books to Read

Armentrout, David, and Patricia Armentrout. *Abraham Lincoln*. Vero Beach, Fla.: Rourke Publishing, 2001.

Binns, Tristan Boyer. *The Lincoln Memorial*. Chicago: Heinemann Library, 2001.

Oberle, Lora Polack. *Abraham Lincoln*. Mankato, Minn.: Capstone Press, 2002.

Places to Visit

Lincoln Home National Historic Site
413 South Eighth Street
Springfield, Illinois 62701
Visitor Information: (217) 492-4241

Lincoln Memorial
National Mall
Washington, D.C. 20024
Visitor Information: (202) 426-6841

Gettysburg National Military Park
97 Taneytown Road
Gettysburg, Pennsylvania 17325
Visitor Information: (717) 334-1124

Index